Sophie and Shine

Kelly McKain

Stripes

For Rob

Special thanks go to our cover stars,
Flora and Schnappy,
Zoe our fab photographer
and Janet Rising for all the
invaluable pony advice.

www.kellymckain.co.uk

STRIPES PUBLISHING
An imprint of Magi Publications
1 The Coda Centre, 189 Munster Road, London SW6 6AW

A paperback original
First published in Great Britain in 2007

Text copyright © Kelly McKain, 2007
Illustrations copyright © Mandy Stanley, 2007
Cover photograph copyright © Zoe Cannon, 2007

ISBN-13: 978-1-84715-020-2

A CIP catalogue record for this book is available from the British Library.

Printed and bound in Belgium by Proost

2 4 6 8 10 9 7 5 3 1

THIS DIARY BELONGS TO

Sophie

Dear Riders,

A warm welcome to Sunnyside Stables!

Sunnyside is our home and for the next week it will be yours too! We're a big family – my husband Johnny and I have two children, Millie and James, plus two dogs ... and all the ponies, of course!

We have friendly yard staff and a very talented instructor, Sally, to help you get the most out of your week. If you have any worries or questions about anything at all, just ask. We're here to help, and we want your holiday to be as enjoyable as possible – so don't be shy!

As you know, you will have a pony to look after as your own for the week. Your pony can't wait to meet you and start having fun! During your stay, you'll be caring for your pony, improving your riding, enjoying long country hacks, learning new skills and making friends.

And this week's special activity is a day out riding in a beautiful horse-drawn carriage! Add swimming, games, films, barbecues and a gymkhana and you're in for a fun-filled holiday to remember!

This special Pony Camp Diary is for you to fill with all your holiday memories. We hope you'll write all about your adventures here at Sunnyside Stables – because we know you're going to have lots!

Wishing you a wonderful time with us!

Jody xx

Monday afternoon
– I'm at Pony Camp!

We've just had lunch on my very first day at Pony Camp, and I thought I'd start writing in my fab new diary straight away. Jody, who runs Sunnyside Stables, gave us one each to write all our adventures in while we're here and I've had such an exciting time already! We had our assessment lesson this morning and I've been given the best pony ever. She's called Shine and she's absolutely gorgeous! I'll write more about her in a minute but I'm going to start right at the beginning so I don't miss anything out.

We were a bit late arriving because my baby brother Albie was screaming and Dad couldn't get him strapped into the car seat. Plus, Mum had to pack all his stuff, like his bottles and nappies and pushchair, and even with me helping it took ages. Albie needs as much for one car journey as I do for a week!

So by the time we got here everyone else was already unpacked and on the yard. Jody showed me upstairs and I had to quickly dump my stuff in the room where I'm staying. I took the top bunk, as someone's towel and nightie were already on the bottom one. There was also an unmade bed by the window covered in soft toy ponies, and Jody told me it belonged to her daughter, Millie.

I hurried down to the yard and Sally the head instructor gave us a welcome talk, and introduced all the yard staff. Then Jody told us

about bedtimes and meals and stuff, and said
to come to her if we had any problems or
questions. Jody's really nice and though she's
Millie's actual mum, she's going to be like a
mum to all of us while we're staying here.

Then Sally got us to introduce ourselves to
each other and I found out that the
other girl (on the bunk below me) is
called Beth. She's my age but a bit
smaller than me, and she's got lovely
wavy hair (I'm always trying to get
mine to go like that but it never
does!). She looked a bit nervous and asked me
if I'd done much riding before.

Beth

I explained that while I've been riding for
quite a few years, I don't get to go very often
any more because of Mum and Dad being so
busy with Albie. "So I've done lots of flatwork
and some jumping but I've probably forgotten
loads of it," I told her. "Actually, that's one of the

things I'm most looking forward to on this holiday – working on my riding non-stop for a whole week!" Then I suddenly panicked thinking what if Millie and Beth are really good, but Beth said, "I've done way less than you – I only started a few months ago, when me and Dad moved down here."

We both turned to Millie at the exact same time and said, "I bet you're brilliant," which was so spooky it made all three of us collapse into giggles. Millie said, "I've been riding a long time, but if I can get my pony to do what I want it's a miracle." Her pony's called Tally and she says his main hobby is bombing off on hacks and dragging her through hedges.

Sunnyside Stables

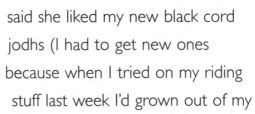

The other girls are lovely too, and I especially like Shanice. She's really smiley and said she liked my new black cord jodhs (I had to get new ones because when I tried on my riding stuff last week I'd grown out of my old ones!). Shanice lives in London and she's hardly ridden at all, but she's so pony mad she saved up for a really nice grooming kit to use on her pony this week. She got given a cute piebald called Prince and she fell in love with him straight away.

The three older girls are really cool. Aneela has amazingly long shiny hair and Izzy's got a fab purple silk she bought specially for this week. Courtney's wearing make-up and when I said I liked her eyeshadow she offered to do a makeover on me one night! Her mum's

actually a beauty therapist so Courtney's learnt
all about make-up and hair and face packs and
stuff from her. Who haven't I mentioned yet?

Oh, yes, Daisy and Grace are the
youngest, they're identical twins
and even their riding gear is
exactly the same (I don't know
how we'll ever tell them apart!).
After a quick tour round the
yard, we were all given our ponies. It
was so exciting waiting to hear who I'd got.
Sally read our names off a list as Lydia brought
the ponies out one by one, and that's when I
met my gorgeous Shine! Lydia had tacked up
the ponies for us this once but we'll be doing
that ourselves for the rest of the week. It's so
great that we get to do everything for them as
well as all the riding. It's almost like actually
owning one. I used to ask and ask and ask
Mum and Dad if I could have my own pony,

but they kept saying no, so I stopped eventually. But it's still my number one dream and I secretly think about it a lot and imagine what it would be like.

Shine's exactly the sort of pony I've been dreaming about! She's a really pretty bay and so sweet and friendly. At 13.2hh she's the perfect size for me too! She's got a beautiful glossy coat and I'm going to make it gleam for the gymkhana on Friday. I feel so lucky that I got her!

I've brought my digital camera and I've taken pix of everyone and their ponies, but there's nowhere here to print them off, so instead I'll have to do some drawings of us all. I know, I'll make it into a puzzle.

Sunnyside Stables

Me

Monsoon

Shine

Shanice

Mischief

Prince

Daisy

Beth

Twinkle

Grace

Cracker

Millie

Izzy

Flame

Charm

Aneela

Tally

Courtney

16

As we were given our ponies, we led them over to the mounting block and got on, ready for the assessment lesson. I had to walk Shine away from the crowd a bit before sorting out my stirrups. She wasn't that keen on standing right near the others and she kept on swishing her tail and shifting about.

It felt strange being back on a pony at first, but in the assessment lesson we had a good long walk round on each rein, so I had time to think about my position and get used to Shine. We did lots of halts, circles and changes of direction to get our ponies listening to us. It took me a while to remember to look around to see where I was going, though! Shine is quite forward-going in trot so I could go rising in a nice rhythm without nagging her all the time. Sally called out to me to change my trot diagonal, though, and I realized I'd forgotten to even check it!

When we had a canter I slid my outside leg back and Shine did as I asked straight away. I'd forgotten how fast it felt – but also how fun! Sally had to tell me to sit back and down, and stop clinging to the reins, but I didn't really mind her saying that because she yells things out to everyone. Shanice hasn't cantered before so she had a trot instead, and Sally said she'd be cantering by the end of the week, no worries. It's great that things are coming back to me already – and it helps that Shine's so lovely to ride! It was just so exciting – and to think, I've got loads more canters to go before the end of the week!

Afterwards we untacked (I helped Shanice with Prince as she hadn't done it before), and then we all gathered back on the yard to hear what groups we'd be in. Sally said I was borderline but she's putting me in Group A to start off with (the beginners' group) so I can find my feet and brush up my skills. If I do well she's going to move me up to Group B. I'm really disappointed to be honest, and can't help thinking that if Mum and Dad hadn't been so busy with Albie... Still, I suppose moving groups can be a goal for me to work towards.

We then had a lecture about safety on the yard and Lydia showed us where everything was and how to put things away properly so nothing got tripped over or lost. It was fun because she pretended to do dangerous things like mounting without her chin strap done up, or tying up a pony without using a slip-knot, and we had to stop her by calling out "No!" and saying what was wrong.

Then at lunch Aneela was doing impressions of a teacher at her riding school at home who has this really snooty voice and we were all in stitches. She's so funny – in fact, all the girls here are nice. We've just been trying on each others' stuff. Daisy's blue fleece really suited Shanice and Izzy's purple silk looked great on Courtney's hat, and she said she really wishes she'd bought a new one before she came, too. Grace insisted on trying on Aneela's jodhs and of course they were miles too long for her! I know I'm going to have a fab week with them all!

COURTNEY wearing IZZY'S silk

Jody just gave us our welcome letters (I've stuck mine in the front of this diary) and we found out we're going carriage-driving this week – we're all really excited. It'll be great fun going on a trip together and only Izzy has been in a carriage before, when she was a bridesmaid at her cousin's wedding, so it'll be a brand new horsey experience too!

We've got to go back on the yard again now for our first Pony Care lecture – it's on tack and tacking up. I'm going to pay extra special attention in the lectures because maybe if I show Mum and Dad how much I've learnt they'll understand how serious I am about getting my own pony, and then they might start to think about it at least.

Monday after dinner

Our lecture was really interesting – we learnt about all the different bits of tack, then watched Lydia demonstrate tacking up on Aneela's pony, Charm. She chose him because he's so good at standing still on the yard. Everyone laughed when Millie said that if we'd used Tally it would have been more like a demonstration of chasing an escaping pony down the lane!

Then we had our first go at tacking up our ponies. Millie has done all this before, so went round helping the younger girls. We did it in their stables and pens to make it easier, and we worked in twos so we could help each other. I went with Beth and she was really good about helping me get the bit in (I've only done it once before and I didn't want to bang poor

Shine's teeth with it). When I helped her with
Monsoon we played this game pretending they
were our own ponies and we were getting
ready for a big comp, and it was really cool.
Beth is so much fun! When Lydia came round
and checked what we'd done all she had to do
was move Shine's girth up a hole, so we were
really happy!

Our lesson this afternoon was fun too. Jody
wanted us to just relax and get to know our
ponies, so we did lots of transitions and
changes of rein to get good control and then
we practised weaving in and out of cones. It
was so funny when Cracker decided he
couldn't be bothered to go round all the cones

and just carted Grace off to the end of the manège instead!

I also found out that Shine gets spooked easily! It was really windy this afternoon and during the lesson a shed door banged and sent her skittering off across the manège. It really freaked me out, and my heart went all fluttery, but I managed to keep going and put her straight. But then she kept refusing to walk past the bit of fence where it happened and Jody said I had to ride really positively so Shine didn't go completely silly about it. I felt really nervous but I made myself act calm and after a while Shine was fine again. Jody called out, "You may not have ridden for a while, Sophie, but you obviously have a feel for ponies. You handled that very well!"

At this rate, maybe I really will get moved up to Group B sometime this week! When we had a canter, Shanice decided to trot again instead and Jody gave her a big smile and said maybe she can have another go tomorrow.

Oh, I nearly forgot. Something strange happened before, when we were doing yard duties. We all put our hard hats on the bench in the tack room so we didn't have to take them upstairs, and I volunteered to sweep the main yard so I could look at Shine, because her stable is right there. When the jobs were done and Sally said it was time to go in for dinner, we all went to pick up our hats. On the way in to the farmhouse, Izzy was asking everyone if they'd seen her silk (the really nice purple one), because it's vanished. It was on her hat when she left it in the tack room but when she went back after yard duties, her hat was just black, and the silk was nowhere to be seen.

Millie said not to worry, and that it probably got lost behind something, and she's sure it'll turn up. But I think it's strange. I mean, how could Izzy's silk have come off the hat on its own?

Weird!

I like mysteries, so I am thinking of ideas about what could have happened. Like, maybe a girth strap caught on the silk while someone was putting their saddle away and pulled it off (not very likely, I know, but it's the best I can think of so far!).

Anyway, I have to go now because we're going swimming for our evening activity (there's a pool here – Millie is just so lucky!).

Monday night in bed,

I'm quickly writing this by the light of my torch.

Swimming was really fun – Millie's dad Johnny organized some water races and games, and then we had time to just play around. Me, Millie and Beth pretended to be synchronized swimmers and made up this whole routine (and completely got the giggles, too!).

Afterwards, when we'd had our showers and dried off, we all had hot chocolate together in the kitchen. This really is turning out to be the perfect holiday!

Millie and Beth and me have all been whispering for the last hour, till they both fell asleep. Beth was telling us how her mum still lives in Manchester and how she hardly ever gets to see her. She's got no brothers and sisters so it's just her and her dad. She says it's fine and she doesn't mind, but I felt really sorry for her – I can't imagine not having Mum around, even if she does spend most of her time with Albie at the moment. Thinking of not having Mum around all the time has made me start missing her, so I'm going to turn off my torch and try to get some sleep before I get really homesick! Goodnight!

Tuesday, we just had lunch, and I want to quickly write about my fab morning!

I had such a great time with Shine this morning, and Jody's lesson was really fun. She's even nice when she's telling you how to correct something. Like, this morning, I wasn't sitting back and down enough in my canter, and she called out, "Sophie, if you keep leaning on the reins I'll make you do it without them!" and everyone laughed.

Sally's group rides in the next manège and she quite often yells at them, not in a nasty way or anything but just kind of shouting, "Leg, leg, leg!" so it's a bit more strict than in our group. I'm still hoping to move up this week, though!

Oh, and Shanice cantered this morning! She held the pommel the first time to get her confidence and then she had another go with just the reins. She was grinning all over her face when Prince came to a stop, and she gave him a big pat to say well done.

It was brilliant at the end of the lesson too because Jody had us doing round-the-worlds as fast as we could – Beth was great at it, and we were all amazed by her whizzing legs, especially as she's only been riding a few months! But she said she used to be in the gymnastics team at her old school, so that explains it! Then we did riding with our arms out to the sides (as in with no reins) to help with our balance. Cracker kept wandering off across the manège, even though Grace was really using her legs, and that had us all giggling.

After our break, we went to the barn for a lecture. It was all about grooming and Daisy brought out some ribbons she'd bought specially to put in Twinkle's tail for the gymkhana (there's a tack and turnout comp as well as the races and stuff). She asked Lydia to show us how to do a tail plait as well as a full groom, so we all got to see how it was done.

The ribbons looked very smart tied on the end of the plait and Lydia did it really, really neatly, so now we all want our ponies to look like that for the gymkhana! She borrowed Shanice's lovely brushes for the grooming demonstration and then when we did our own ponies, everyone was asking if they could borrow them too. I brought Shine into the barn to be with the other ponies (most of them are turned out at night), and after we'd given them a thorough groom we had a go at the tail plaiting. It was much, much harder than it looked and mine came out a bit wrong, but Courtney helped me to sort it out. She was really good at it and her fingers were flicking over and under and the plait got longer and longer at lightning speed. I even had to get her to slow down so I could see what she was doing. She said that her mum does French plaits for weddings and they're not all that different to tail plaits for ponies! There's still plenty of time for me to practise before Friday, luckily!

Tuesday, it's our free time after dinner (we had sausages and mash!)

 *Yum!*

Oh dear, another strange thing has happened and now I don't know what to think. Millie and Beth are on washing-up duty at the moment (I'm on tomorrow with Shanice), so I've got a bit of time to write about it in my diary.

But first, let me just write about the fab pony stuff we did this afternoon. To start with we had a lecture about road safety and first aid, and what to do if you get lost on a hack (which is find a landmark if possible and then call the yard for help), and then we actually went out on one all together! Me, Millie and

Beth chattered all the way round, apart from when we had to concentrate on trotting up the hills and going through this river without coming off and getting very wet! I really wish Millie and Beth lived near me so we could hang round together all the time. And I wish Shine could be my pony for ever!

Then, when we got back, the strange thing happened. After the hack, we were untacking and doing yard duties, and when I went to put Shine's bridle back in the tack room, I found Daisy searching through her tack box with Grace and Shanice. They explained that

Twinkle's ribbons had gone missing. Daisy looked a bit upset so I gave her a hug and said, "Don't worry, we'll find them."

While they searched all over the tack room and the yard, I went back to the barn where we'd had the demonstration in case the ribbons had fallen into the straw. As I stood there, I remembered something that hadn't seemed at all important this morning. I'd noticed that while we were packing away, Daisy's ribbons *did* fall into the straw. I was about to go and get them for her when Courtney picked them up. I turned to get my hoof pick from Grace and of course I just assumed that Courtney put them back in Daisy's tack box, but what if she hadn't? They certainly aren't there now. What if Courtney thought no one was looking and sneaked them into her pocket instead? Oh, that can't be true, can it?

Suddenly I found myself thinking about Izzy's purple silk as well, which still hasn't turned up. Courtney was the one who tried it on her hat when we were swapping stuff yesterday. But surely she couldn't have taken it – and Daisy's ribbons. Could she?

When I got back to the tack room the ribbons still hadn't been found, though.

"Listen, don't worry, Mum's got a big box of ribbons for everyone to use for the gymkhana," Millie was telling Daisy. "If yours don't turn up, you can choose some new ones from there. We'll let you have first pick, won't we, girls?" We all nodded and Daisy cheered up a bit after that.

Millie seems convinced that Daisy's ribbons just got lost somewhere, but I'm not so sure.

After dinner just now, when we were all

clearing the plates away, I got up the courage to ask Courtney if she'd seen Daisy's ribbons in the barn at the end of the lecture. She didn't even look startled or anything and she just said, "Yeah, I did. They'd fallen into the straw so I just picked them up and put them back in her tack box. They must have gone missing after that." I was silent for a moment, thinking, and she gave me a funny look and said, "Why do you ask?" I quickly shook my head and mumbled, "No reason."

Luckily I can stop thinking about it now because it's time to go outside. We were going to have a film tonight because of the rain but it's stopped now so we're playing rounders instead. I hope my team wins!

Still Tuesday, just!

Millie and Beth are asleep, but I feel wide awake after what just happened. I'm worried Millie thinks I'm a bit horrible or something. I wasn't going to say anything, but we had such a good time playing rounders together (we didn't win, but never mind!) and then whispering after lights out, that it just sort of came out.

First, I made them promise not to tell anyone, and then I told them about how I'd seen Courtney pick up the ribbons in the barn, but that I wasn't sure if she really had put them into Daisy's tack box. And I reminded them that Courtney was the one who'd really liked the purple silk, too.

They were both silent for a long time and I started to wish I hadn't said anything. Then

Millie said, "But Sophie, we were all admiring Izzy's silk in the yard, and Courtney did say she'd put the ribbons back when you asked her."

"Yeah, I suppose so," I mumbled. "Beth? What do you think?" I whispered then, but there was no reply. What a shame she'd fallen asleep just when I needed her to back me up.

Millie sighed loudly. "Look, the silk could have been pulled off Izzy's hat by accident and fallen down somewhere," she whispered. "And as for Daisy's ribbons, they could have blown out of her tack box as she came back across the yard, and maybe even been swept up by now. You can't just accuse someone – you have to be sure."

I didn't say anything after that. I just lay here, feeling really awkward. After a while Millie fell asleep so I found my torch and got out my diary. Oh, I really hope she doesn't think badly of me for mentioning it. And I'm glad Beth didn't hear me after all. Us three get on so well, it would be awful if we fell out over this!

I feel a bit better now I've written all that down. I'm going to try to sleep, so that the morning comes quicker and I can see Shine again. Jody says we're off on our carriage-driving trip tomorrow too – I'm really looking forward to that!

It's our free time
after lunch on Wednesday

I wolfed down my breakfast this morning so I could be first out for yard duty. I couldn't wait to see Shine and have a private talk to her about what happened last night. After filling a few of the water buckets for Lydia, I got on with giving Shine a good groom before tacking up. As I combed Shine's mane, I told her all about the silk and the ribbons in a low voice. I was careful that no one overheard, especially because by then the yard was busy with all the girls

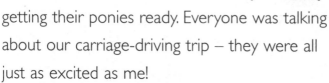

getting their ponies ready. Everyone was talking about our carriage-driving trip – they were all just as excited as me!

When I'd told Shine everything, she nuzzled into my shoulder, like she was telling me I was right to say something last night after all.

And it turns out I really was — because just then Shanice came running out of the tack room and straight over to Shine's stable. "Sophie, my body brush, from my grooming kit, it's disappeared!" she wailed, tears in her eyes.

"Are you sure?" I asked. She nodded miserably. "I cleaned my kit and put it away before dinner yesterday," she mumbled. "I even double checked I had everything because I'd been lending things out."

I came out of Shine's stable and put my arm round her, and Millie, Daisy, Grace and Beth hurried over to find out what was wrong (the older girls were busy helping Lydia in the top barn). As Shanice explained, I gave Millie a meaningful look. She frowned and said, "Okay, it does look like something funny is going on. Let's go to Mum."

So we all marched off to the kitchen and told Jody about the brush. We also mentioned the silk not turning up, and about Daisy's ribbons going missing. I felt so sorry for Shanice and I really wanted to tell Jody what I suspected about Courtney, too, but Millie gave me a sharp look and mouthed the words "no proof". She's right, there isn't any, so I'll just have to find a way to get some. I really think Courtney is stealing things now and I can't let her get away with it.

I felt loads better when Jody took charge. She sent Millie to ask the yard staff if anyone had borrowed the brush in the evening without putting it back (they hadn't). And she asked Beth to go up to the top barn to bring

back the older girls, and then got us to check
all the Sunnyside tack boxes in case it had
somehow been put back in the wrong one.
We also looked in every stable, the office, the
barns and the house. When none of the things
were found, Jody just stood frowning for a
moment, thinking. Then she snapped out of it.
"Right, girls, I'm sure we'll sort this out," she
said briskly. "On a brighter note, Sophie, you're
moving into Group B this morning. Well done
for improving so much."

I couldn't believe it! I've done it! I've been
moved up!

Everyone gave me a clap, which was
so cool, and I couldn't help beaming. Then we
had to hurry up and finish tacking up for our
lessons, because we were running a bit late
after hunting for the brush.

My first lesson in Group B didn't go that
well, actually. I was a bit nervous that I wouldn't

be able to do what the others could, and of letting Sally down, and I think Shine picked up on that. She was really skittish, and after she knocked down a pole on the jump we were popping, she kept spooking and running out at the last minute. Sally told me to try again and again, so Shine wouldn't think that being naughty was going to get her out of jumping. I didn't really want to because I felt like it wasn't Shine's fault she didn't want to pop the jump, and that she was honestly scared. I wouldn't even give her a tap with the crop before going over, as Sally had asked me to.

Instead, I just kept failing and I got more and more flustered until Sally told me to come into the middle and take a break. I did have another go and I got Shine over in the end, but I felt so annoyed with myself. Sally must think I'm a rubbish rider!

At least it wasn't as if everyone in Group B was riding perfectly (which is what I'd imagined!). When we did

ME *getting* **FLUSTERED**

some sitting trot, Izzy lost her hold on the reins and Mischief took advantage, cutting the corner off, and Aneela was bobbling around clutching Charm's mane. Courtney called out, "Ow, my bum!" and everyone else laughed, but I didn't feel like joining in, I couldn't stop thinking about what she'd done.

Anyway, after a while in sitting trot I
remembered to let my legs and seat bones go
soft. Once I'd stopped trying to grip on I got
into a good rhythm and it was like my bum
was glued to the seat – for a few strides
anyway! I was hoping Sally would notice and
she did, saying, "Well done, Sophie, lovely!" I'm
glad she's seen me do one thing well, anyway. I
can't wait to show Mum and Dad how much
I've improved this week!

And the lecture was the best one we've had
yet! It was called 'All About Ponies' and
covered everything from points of the horse
to colour and markings, conformation and
breeds. I acted silly to make Shanice laugh and
help take her mind off the missing brush.

Lydia obviously had the same idea as me
about cheering Shanice up because she asked
her to get Prince out of the barn to be the
demonstration pony, and let her hold him

while she showed us the points of the horse.

Aneela was really sweet to Shanice as well, and she lent her this cool pink and purple stripy lead rope to bring Prince out with. I'm determined to catch the thief (you know who!) and get Shanice her brush back, but I don't know how. I'll have to try and come up with a plan!

Anyway, after the demonstration bit, it was really fun because we went round the yard in twos seeing how many markings we could spot. Me and Shanice spent ages trying to

work out whether Shine has a big snip or a
short stripe! In the end we decided that she's
so special and unique that maybe there isn't
even a name for her marking, so we made one
up — a strinip!

I have to stop writing, we're off on our trip
now. I've never been in a carriage before and
I can't wait! I wonder if it will be a
grand one like they sometimes
have in those old-fashioned
shows on TV, or more like a
farm cart, or even a racing
chariot! I wonder what the
horses and ponies will be like and
if we'll get to help put the harnesses
and stuff on them. I wonder … oh, I guess
I'll just have to wait and see!

'strinip'

Wednesday at 4.30pm

We're in the minibus on our way back from the carriage driving. Lydia says I'll make myself feel sick, writing on the move, but I don't want to forget anything about the trip because it was brilliant!

It took about half an hour to get to the farmhouse (Johnny drove us, and Lydia came too). When we got there, we met Fred and his wife, Marjorie, who are total carriage-driving fanatics. They took us round the barns, and showed us all their different coaches and traps and things. Some were really shiny and perfect and some were all in bits (Fred's hobby is restoring them). When he pointed out the trap we'd be riding in — a two-wheeler that only fitted one person and the driver, we got even more excited. Marjorie explained that we couldn't drive it ourselves because it's not a skill you can just learn in half an hour, but if we were lucky she might give us a little go of the steering. So we practised with these reins that were attached to the wall in the barn. It's really different to normal riding because you put both reins in your left hand and just use your right as a guide.

We were all laughing because, well, for a start we were driving a wall, and also, when we got it wrong Marjorie was making up pretend things that would happen if we really did steer like that, saying, "Your horse would be in the ditch right now," or "You'd have hit a tree by the side of the road!"

Then we walked over to the stables and everyone went really crazy over the horses and ponies. There was a pair of greys a bit like Jody's mare, Bonny, which pull carriages as a

51

team, and a pair of black horses that Fred
called Hackneys – a breed that's really good at
trotting. Then we met the pony that we were
going to be driving – a gorgeous cobby gelding
called Bayleaf – and everyone went even more
crazy over him.

There are loads of different straps and
things on a driving harness and Marjorie said it
all has to go on in the right order or it's
unlucky. There's a saddle, just like in normal
riding, but it looks really different, like this:

Carriage
Saddle

NOT FOR
SITTING ON!

Also, the pony
wears blinkers to stop him from looking
behind at the carriage and you have to be
really careful to make sure the blinkers fit
properly. If they don't they could rub on the

pony's eyes or gape so that he could see behind him after all and get scared by the trap.

When Bayleaf was all ready, Fred held him while Marjorie attached the trap, and then we all had a turn of sitting up in the carriage with her. It was so brilliant trotting up and down the lane, and Marjorie let me have a little go at the steering too! It's weird because you can't use your legs and seat (obviously!) but only your hands and voice (they do use a whip sometimes but I couldn't manage that as well!). It's amazing to think that in the old days most transport was actually horse-drawn, so you would have ridden in a carriage or a trap everyday. Mum would have had to let me get my own pony then. It would have been just as normal as having a car!

I couldn't get the hang of the steering at first and Bayleaf went a bit slow and wobbly, but I soon got him going again. It was such a great feeling rattling along the lane with the sound of his hooves clip-clopping and the wheels clattering. Then Marjorie took over the steering and she got Bayleaf going so fast the carriage was really bouncing along. It was way better than the best fairground ride and I just couldn't stop grinning.

When we'd all had a go in the trap, we had a drink and some of Marjorie's home-made apple cake – yum! Then Fred took us to see one special coach he was restoring, which was in a barn on its own. It was really grand and a few of us could sit in it at once. I pretended to be in a film where they wear all the old-style costumes, like in Victorian times, and then the other girls joined in, and Lydia acted the part of our governess and really made us laugh by inspecting our fingernails and everything.

Oh, hang on, I do feel a bit sick actually – I'd better stop writing for now!

Wednesday at 8.16pm

I ♥ this HOLIDAY!

We've just been swimming again and everyone's milling around getting showered and dressed. I'm just waiting for Millie and Beth to leave the room so I can sneak out unnoticed. I've got a fab plan to catch you-know-who in the act of taking something else and I'm going to put it into action.

I thought of it when we got back to the yard this afternoon. We had some time with our ponies, mucking out the stables and barn and topping up their water and everything. I was just telling Shine how I needed a plan to catch the thief when something happened to give me the answer.

I was about to take my barrow to the muck heap when Lydia came along. She nudged the bolt over on the bottom of Shine's door with her foot. "Don't forget the kick bolt, Sophie," she said, smiling. "Some of the ponies have a habit of sneaking out! In fact, one morning there was so much hay missing we had to set up a watch in the office overnight to find the culprits."

I laughed and asked who they were.

"Cracker and Mischief," she said. "As I'd guessed. They're out in the field now, of course, but over the winter we really have to watch them. Cracker was getting very tubby and we just couldn't understand why!"

Then Lydia walked off and I started sweeping again, but when I looked up at Shine she was really staring at me, like she was trying to tell me something. I leaned on my broom and stared back at her. "What is it,

Shine?" I asked, and she just kept looking at me. Then I realized – Lydia has given me the perfect idea.

I'm going to set up a watch of my own, like she did, but not from the office, obviously. Shine's stable will make the perfect hiding place and plus, she can keep me company – we'll be a detective team! It won't be all night either, as Jody checks on us at about quarter past 9 and the activities don't finish till just after 8. I know that if Courtney sneaks back out here it would have to be between those times because she'd be missed before or after. Shanice's brush was definitely there when we went in for dinner, after all, and wasn't there in the morning so that's the only time it could have been stolen.

I wanted to run and tell Beth and Millie about my plan, but then I remembered how Millie reacted before so I've decided to do it alone, and only tell them after I've got the proof.

I've also been thinking about what's been taken so far and trying to work out what Courtney might go for next (if she comes out at all, that is). At first, I couldn't see the point of her taking those things.

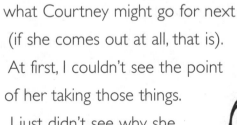

I just didn't see why she would. I mean, if she actually used the ribbons, we'd all notice, and how would she explain suddenly having a new silk to her mum? She doesn't have her own pony so why would she need a body brush?

Then I realized – they're all things the girls were really proud of and that everyone said were nice. It's like she's taking things that get their owners lots of attention. Plus, they've all been taken from the tack room. Courtney obviously doesn't want to risk stealing from the

bedrooms, where she might easily be caught.
So, I have a hunch she'll go for Aneela's
stripy lead rope next, because
everyone's been saying how nice
it is and asking where she got it.

I hate sneaking around like
this, but I really need to get proof before
I go to Jody. Okay, I'm going out now. I'm taking
my digital camera with me to catch Courtney
in the act. Millie's busy in the kitchen and I
think Beth's with her, or she might be on the
phone in the hall downstairs. Anyway, I'll have
to go now before they come back or it'll be
too late.

7.20am on Thursday morning,
before the others have woken up

I'm sitting up in bed writing this.

Well, I wasn't expecting…

I still can't believe it…

Oh, I don't know where to start. Maybe I should just write everything down from where I left off.

Well, I sneaked out to the yard and I was in Shine's stable waiting with my camera. After a while, I heard someone coming right past Shine's door, so I had to duck down. As I bobbed back up again, I saw the tack room door swinging shut. I slipped out and hurried across to it, trying not to make a sound. Then I threw the door open, camera ready to catch Courtney in the act. She swung round, Aneela's stripy lead rope in her hand.

And that's when I got the shock of my life.

It wasn't Courtney, but Beth. As in my *friend* Beth.

She froze, staring at me, and the lead rope slithered to the floor.

"Beth! What are you doing with…" I began, but she just stared at me. "Oh, you had the same idea as me," I said then. "You were going to catch the thief too."

But Beth shook her head. Her shoulders slumped and she stared at the floor. "Sophie, I … I didn't mean to…" she mumbled.

I suddenly understood what she was saying and it made me shiver. I could hardly believe it. Could Beth really be the thief? "But Courtney…" I began.

"No," said Beth. "She didn't take the ribbons."

"So you did hear what I said to Millie!" I cried.

Beth nodded miserably. "Yes, but I didn't know what to say so I pretended to be asleep. And yes, Courtney did put the ribbons back in Daisy's tack box, but I took them out again." Her voice cracked and she started to cry.

"But, how could you take our things?" I demanded. "Especially Shanice's brush, when she saved up so hard and everything. And Daisy was really upset…"

Beth was sobbing by then and part of me wanted to go and give her a hug, but I also felt furious. "You're my friend," I said. "I can't believe you'd do something like this."

Beth sat down heavily on a pile of numnahs waiting for the wash. "I didn't really mean to," she gabbled. "It just sort of happened. I was in the tack room on my own and I decided to try Izzy's silk on my hat, just for a minute. So I took it off hers but then I heard people coming and I didn't know what to do, so I shoved it in my pocket and hurried back on to the yard. I was going to put it back later, but there wasn't a good time. When she saw it was missing I didn't know how to explain so I sort of ended up keeping it."

I sighed. "But what about Daisy's ribbons and Shanice's brush? You can't say you didn't mean to take those too."

Beth's shoulders slumped further. "I don't know," she mumbled. "I just felt really sort of … almost, like, jealous of them…"

"You mean, because they got attention for having those nice things?" I suggested.

Beth thought for a moment then nodded miserably and wiped her eyes on the sleeve of her fleece. "Everyone else seems to get noticed and not me," she sniffled. "Like with Dad, I feel invisible since he got this new girlfriend, Sarah. There's no time for me, I'm just in the way. It's obvious they'd rather do things on their own. And now he's asked her to move in with us and I don't, I don't…"

I was really surprised. "But you said everything was fine between you and your dad," I stuttered.

"It was … before Sarah came along. I had to pretend to Dad that everything was all right, but secretly I kept hoping that they'd split up and things would go back to being the way they were: just the two of us."

"Well, maybe they will," I said.

But Beth shook her head. "It's not going to happen. Just before I came here I found out she's moving in. I didn't say anything to you and Millie because I didn't want to even think about it during my holiday."

Then she dissolved into tears again. This
time I went and sat down next to her.
"Come on, it's not as bad
as all that," I said stiffly.
"Why don't you just
tell your dad how
you feel?"

"I tried to," she half-
whispered, "but then I found myself saying I
was okay because I didn't want him to be
upset with me."

"I know how you feel," I admitted. "I was
happy with things as they were – just as me,
Mum and Dad. But then when they had Albie
it was like I didn't exist, apart from to do
chores and clean up after him. And they're
always too tired to do anything. But I can't tell
them I wish it was the three of us again –
Mum would be so upset."

Beth leaned against my shoulder then and I didn't shrug her off. We both sat there quietly for a while, thinking. I did feel sorry for her, but I couldn't forget what she'd done. "Just because you're having a hard time, that doesn't mean you can steal things," I said, firmly.

"I know," she replied. "It's not an excuse. It was wrong and I should never have done it. I'm really not like that, honest." She started crying again then, and said, "Please believe me."

"Look, I do believe you, but you have to talk to your dad about how you feel," I told her. "But first you have to put things right here."

"I'll put everything back the first chance I get," she sniffled. "I promise. But…" Beth looked up at me, and even in the half light I could see that she was nervous and scared. "You won't tell on me, will you, Sophie?" she almost-whispered. I thought about

66

what might happen – a thief would probably
be sent home in disgrace. Beth's dad would be
furious. I didn't know what to do. I still don't. I
mean, she's stolen things from my friends. I
should tell, shouldn't I? But then, she was so
upset, and I do believe she's sorry.

I didn't say yes or no, instead I just told her
to go back in. She nodded, wiped her tears
away and stumbled out of the tack room. I
watched her dash round the side of the
stables. When she'd gone, I slipped out too and
turned to go the same way. But just then Lydia
came out of the office. I couldn't run for the
corner, it was too far. I just sort of froze as she
walked up to me. "Sophie? What are you doing
out here?" she asked.

"Erm, nothing," I said quickly.

She frowned at me in the dusky light,
following my nervous glance to the tack room
door, which was half open.

"I, er, I couldn't resist coming out to see
Shine, and I thought I'd just
check the tack room for,
er…" I couldn't think of
what I possibly needed to
check in the tack room for. It
was a fib and Lydia knew it.

"Well, you shouldn't be out. Off you go," she
said.

I hurried back to the farmhouse, heart
pounding, and I could feel her watching me as I
turned the corner by the stables, but I didn't
dare look back.

I went straight into the shower, then joined
everyone else downstairs for hot chocolate.

Luckily Beth had her shower after me, so I
managed to avoid her, and when she came
down for her hot chocolate I went upstairs,
saying how tired I was. So when my room-
mates came up I was already in bed,

pretending to be asleep. I didn't want Beth to ask me again whether I was going to tell or not, because I hadn't decided. I still haven't (while I was thinking with my eyes shut I actually fell asleep for real).

And I still don't know what to do about Beth. I mean, how can we be friends now I know what she's done? Surely I should only care about Shanice and the other girls' feelings and not Beth's? Yes, she's promised to put everything back, and I really think she will, but is that enough?

Right, I've decided I'm going to tell. Oh, but what if Beth gets sent home in disgrace? That would be awful, and her dad would be so angry with her.

Oh wait, I think Beth's waking up. I'll go and wash my face in the bathroom so we don't have to talk.

Thursday morning still

I'm writing this in the games room, while everyone's finishing their breakfast.

When I got back from the bathroom I couldn't avoid Beth any more. Millie went back downstairs to give Jody a hand with the breakfast, so it was just the two of us. I pretended to be busy folding my clothes, not looking at her.

"Sophie," she began, "I know you have to do what you think is right, but I've been so worried I've hardly slept. Are you going to talk to Jody about what I've done?"

I sighed and looked up. She was so upset, I knew I couldn't make it worse by telling. "Well, I really should … but no," I said.

Beth looked really relieved. "Thanks! Oh, thanks so much," she gabbled. "It was a mistake,

I promise. It felt awful and I'll never do it again. I'll put everything back today, the very first chance I get to slip out."

"Good," I said, then I grabbed my diary and made for the door. I didn't want to talk about it any more.

"Sophie," she said, and I paused in the doorway. "It's just, well, can we still be friends?" she asked shyly.

"Oh! Erm, I've got to go now," I mumbled and hurried out without looking at her. I don't know if I want to be friends after this, I mean, how could I trust her?

It's time for yard duty now so I'm going to put this diary upstairs and forget all about what's happened. I'm so glad it's over. Beth'll put the stuff back and everything will be normal again and I can just carry on enjoying my holiday with my gorgeous pony.

It's after our lesson now, and I'm hiding in our room.

Everything's gone really wrong and it's hard to write – I'm still trembling from what just happened. I came up here to look for Beth but I can't find her anywhere, so I'm just going to lie on my bed and write this and calm down a bit. I feel like I never want to go downstairs again!

What happened was, after the lesson, Jody came up and asked me to untack Shine quickly and meet her in the kitchen. I'd had trouble with Shine again in Sally's lesson, and so she told me to get tougher, and I'd ended up getting all nervous and flustered. Jody didn't look happy and I thought she'd say I hadn't done well enough in Sally's group and I had to go back into Group A.

But it was worse than that. Much worse.

I got into the kitchen and Jody looked up from the papers on the table in front of her.

"Ah, Sophie," she said. "Thanks for coming in. Look, this is a bit awkward but I have to ask – do you know anything about these things that have gone missing?"

I just stood there feeling completely confused. I couldn't think why she'd ask me especially, on my own. At first I thought she knew about Beth, but then I realized that there's no way she could. She said, "Sophie?" again and I realized I hadn't replied.

"I, er, I don't understand…" I began. Then it hit me – when Lydia saw me, she could have thought I was the thief!

She must have mentioned seeing me last night to Jody. Even though I hadn't actually done anything, I couldn't help blushing.

"I know I was out in the yard when I shouldn't have been, but I'm not a thief!" I cried, feeling panicky. "Please don't think that!"

I really wanted Jody to say, *Of course I don't think that*, but instead she just said, "So there's nothing you want to tell me?"

There was a long silence. I kept my eyes glued to the floor but I could feel her looking at me. My mind was in a whirl of confusion – I couldn't tell on Beth when I'd promised not to, could I? Finally I shook my head. "No, nothing," I mumbled.

"Sophie, I don't want to think badly of you," Jody said then. "But you were seen on the yard when you shouldn't have been, and the tack room door was open. I'm not saying you took those things, but I can't help feeling you're hiding something."

Just then, there was a sound from outside in the hall. Aneela poked her head round the

doorway. Jody put on a forced smile and said, "Could we just have a moment, please?"
Aneela gave me a funny look and I hurriedly stared at the floor again.

Jody sighed, and said, "Well, if you're not going to tell me anything, you'd better go." I couldn't stand the disappointment in her voice. It's awful that she thinks I could have stolen those things. And even worse that she might ring my parents.

My first thought was to find Beth, and tell her things had changed and that she has to own up or I'd get the blame. But when I got to the games room, Millie and Beth weren't there. The other girls were all whispering together and when they saw me

they suddenly stopped. Aneela glared at me
and put her arm round Shanice. She must have
overheard me and Jody in the kitchen, and told
everyone what happened. Now they all think *I*
am the thief! My heart was pounding and I
couldn't even bear to look at Shanice. I just
turned and ran out.

I tried to find Beth in the yard, but she
wasn't with Millie, who was helping Johnny in
the office. She wasn't in the barn with
Monsoon, either. I raced back indoors and
came upstairs, but she's not here.

Oh, she's…

It's still Thursday, but after lunch

I've found a little space round the side of the barn so I can be on my own.

I suddenly had to stop writing earlier because Beth came into our room.

"When Aneela said you… Well, I panicked," she told me, shakily. "I ran up to the top field – I was really scared and I didn't know what to do." She took a deep breath then and said, "But I do now. I've come to get the things I took, and I'm going downstairs right now, to tell everyone the truth. Don't worry, they won't think it was you for long."

She leaned over her bed and rummaged in the bottom corner, under the covers. She pulled out Shanice's brush, and the purple silk and the ribbons. She was very pale and her hands were trembling.

"But what if you get sent home?" I asked. "Won't your dad be really angry?"

Beth's eyes filled with tears but she looked determined. "I'll just have to face that" she said. "You've been such a good friend to me, Sophie, I'm not going to let you down again. I'd better…" And she gestured to the door.

I suddenly found myself standing up. "I'll come with you," I said.

She smiled a watery smile. "Thanks."

So we went down to the games room together, Beth clutching the stolen things. The other girls were all chatting and Jody was there too, clearing the cups and snacks away.

"Jody, I've got something to tell you," Beth began, and then burst into tears.

I put my arm round her as she held out the missing things.

Beth didn't need to say anything else. Jody understood straight away. "Oh, Beth," she said, "you have been a silly girl, haven't you?" The other girls gradually fell silent and gathered around us.

"I'm so sorry," Beth said to Izzy, then Daisy, then Shanice as she handed back their things, but none of them said, "That's okay."

For a moment there was an awful silence. Then Izzy mumbled, "She should go home."

We all looked at Jody. She sighed. I could see she was really disappointed in Beth. I was certain she was going to send her home. But then Jody said, "As it's Friday tomorrow and Beth has owned up, she'll be staying to the end of the week. However, I will be speaking privately to her father tomorrow, and she'll be excluded from the hack this afternoon as punishment. Beth, you can do poo-picking in the field instead. Now, why don't you pop upstairs and wash your face?" With that, Beth raced out of the room without looking at anyone.

"Now, come on, time for you all to get back on the yard, there's a lot to do," Jody told us. As I was turning to go, Aneela caught my arm and said, "Sorry for thinking you were the thief, Sophie."

I was going to be cross with her, but then I remembered how I'd done that too, over Courtney and the silk, and I blushed. "That's okay," I told her. I knew how bad she felt because I felt like that too. I should never have jumped to conclusions.

I'm glad no one thinks I'm a thief any more. I just want things to go back to normal, but I don't know if I can be friends with Beth again.

Thursday night, in bed after lights out

We didn't have a lecture this afternoon, just an extra-long hack in the countryside. Beth didn't come as she was poo-picking the upper field, and some of the other girls were saying mean things about her as we rode along, but I didn't want to join in. I thought Beth had been very brave to own up. Millie didn't seem interested in being nasty about Beth, either and instead we just concentrated on having fun. Shine was so brilliant, she really loved being out in the countryside!

When we were going through the woods a bird flew out of the bushes and Shine did her spooky thing of going sideways again. I didn't mind, though, and I just steered her back on to the path without even worrying. I realized that

I just need to do that in the manège, as if it's nothing, and then Shine will behave and I won't get panicky. I'm definitely going to put that into practice tomorrow.

We had a canter across a stubble field too and it was fantastic. Millie stopped holding Tally back and he galloped the whole way – and Shine followed! It was brilliant, just hearing the pounding of their hooves and leaving everyone else behind, even the older girls! Shine got so excited I had to do a circle at the other end of the field to slow her down, before she'd go back into trot, and again I just calmly did it and she got the message. When we finally halted, me and Millie just looked at each other, grinning and catching our breath. In fact, even thinking about it is making me smile now. I did miss Beth a bit, though. It seemed strange just being Millie and me.

When we got back and went in for tea, Beth was already in the kitchen, helping Jody to serve-up. We were all talking about the hack and how much fun we had. But no one really included Beth and when she did try to say something to Izzy and Aneela they just ignored her. Millie and I weren't exactly talking to her either, but I didn't like seeing her so left out. I was really embarrassed when Jody leaned over the table and said, "Come on, girls, everyone makes mistakes, and it took a lot of courage for Beth to own up. So let's put this behind us, shall we? We're here to enjoy our ponies and the riding, remember?"

There was a really awkward silence that went on for ages and ages after that, but

people do seem to be being a bit nicer to
Beth now. After tea, Courtney did my make-up
and she let me practise my tail plaiting on her
hair. After a couple of goes I started getting the
hang of it, so I'm definitely going to try it
out on Shine tomorrow.

This evening we watched a
DVD of famous three-day
eventers at Burghley Horse Trials.
Jody made us popcorn, and we
were glued to the TV, all going "Wow!"
and "Eeek!" together as the eventers cleared
these massive jumps. It was good because Beth
could easily join in and no one was not
speaking to anyone.

I can't believe it's my last day here
tomorrow – and my last ride on Shine! I can't
wait for the gymkhana! I'm going to give Dad
my camera to take loads of pix – and hopefully
I'll win a rosette too!

Friday lunchtime

I'm quickly writing this before our parents arrive and the gymkhana starts!

It's really funny because everyone keeps crashing about up here looking for their hair bobbles and changing their mind about what top to wear and stuff. I got changed really quickly into my smart clothes – I'd planned what I was going to wear for the gymkhana about 3 days before I even got here, I was looking forward to it so much!

We had great fun on the yard just now – we tied all our ponies up next to each other so we could get them ready for this afternoon. We shared the box of ribbons and the quarter-mark stencils and everything, and borrowed things from each other, and it was like a pampering party for ponies.

Here are all the things I did to spruce up Shine for the gymkhana:

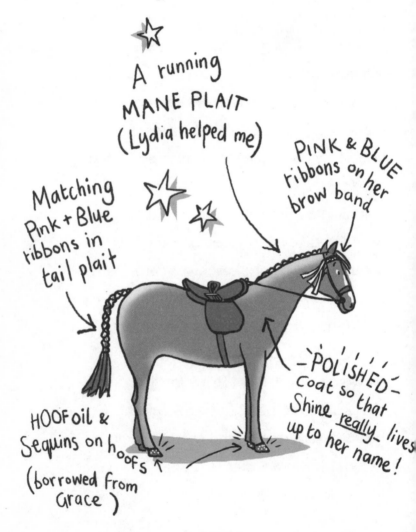

A running
MANE PLAIT
(Lydia helped me)

PINK & BLUE
ribbons on her
brow band

Matching
Pink + Blue
ribbons in
tail plait

-`POLISHED`-
Coat so that
Shine _really_ lives
up to her name!

HOOF oil &
Sequins on hoofs
(borrowed from
Grace)

Then we all cleaned our tack until it was
spotless and gleaming. Hopefully me and Shine
will win the tack and turnout competition after
all that effort, although I have to admit the
other ponies looked fantastic too. Courtney
did some cool chequer-pattern quarter marks
on Flame, and Daisy did the tail plait with
ribbons in it that Lydia showed us on Tuesday.
When she got a bit stuck halfway, Beth offered to
help and Daisy said yes please, so that was good.

When Beth came back over to Monsoon, I
gave her a secret grin and she grinned back.
Yes, I've decided to be friends with her again.
Then Shine stretched her neck and nuzzled
Beth's shoulder, like she was pleased that things
were turning out okay, too.

In our last lesson this morning we had a go
at neck reining, which Sally explained is this
way of putting both reins in one hand and
using the pressure of them against the pony's

neck to steer. She said it makes riding much easier when you're holding things for the gymkhana games, but when we tried it, we all kept going the wrong way and nearly crashing into each other. Sally laughed and said, "On second thoughts, maybe just use both hands on the reins or it's going to be chaos this afternoon!"

We had a go at some of the games we'll be playing too, so that everyone knew what to do. Shine's quite quick at the bending, and all the stuff I've remembered this week about how to use my legs as a pair to keep her straight really helped. I stayed relaxed with her too, and when she tried to skitter about I just kept going as if it didn't bother me. She soon settled down and Sally even noticed and said well done, so that was fab! Let's hope me and Shine win a rosette this afternoon – I've never won anything before and I'd love to have one to stick on my wall!

Sunnyside Stables

Friday dinner time
At home again!

I've only just got home, I haven't even unpacked, but I'm writing this straight away so I don't forget anything.

When my family got here, I was surprised at how pleased I was to see them. Yes, even Albie! All the other girls loved him and it was really cool when they wanted him to grip their fingers and asked me loads of questions about him. I showed Mum, Dad and Albie round the

yard and introduced them to Shine. She was in her stable, all tacked up and ready to go, and Mum and Dad made a big fuss of her. They were really proud when I told them I got moved up a group.

When everyone's parents had arrived it was
time for the gymkhana. I had butterflies in my
stomach but I couldn't stop smiling. The first
thing we did was lead our ponies out of the
stables and into the manège for the tack and
turnout competition. We had to stand next to
them, very straight and tall, and try not to
laugh when Johnny and Lydia came round to
judge. That was quite hard because Lydia
looked under Shine's tail to make sure I'd
cleaned her bottom properly (which I had –
yucky but important!). And when they were
inspecting Cracker he did a wee and Lydia
said, "Well, that's not very gentlemanly, is it?"
and we all burst out giggling.

Of course, I had my fingers crossed for me
and Shine, but I was really pleased for Daisy
when she won. We all gave her a clap and she
took a big bow, and then it was time to mount
up for the games.

What happened was, the Group A people went against each other while we cheered them on and then we had our go while they cheered for us. These are some of the races we did:

Walk, trot, canter – You go up the manège in walk, back in trot and up again in canter. It was so funny in our heat because Tally didn't understand the concept of trying to go slowly, and he kept breaking into trot during the walking bit so he and Millie got sent back to the beginning three times.

Stepping Stones – We had to canter up, then get off and step from straw bale to straw bale while leading our ponies. That was such a fun game!

Ball and racket – We had to balance a ball on a tennis racket and ride steadily enough to keep it there all the way across the manège. Izzy and Millie had no

chance with their boisterous ponies tearing off in canter, but I was doing really well.

Then, Shine spooked at Millie's flying ball and skittered sideways, oh well! Aneela ended up winning on Charm, who's about the best behaved pony you can possibly get. Shanice won the Group A comp on Prince, and I was so pleased for her and clapped extra hard when she got her rosette.

Bending – Guess what? I actually won this one! Shine was brilliant and really listened to my legs.

I was so proud when I got my rosette for the bending, and everyone clapped (and Dad took loads of pix!). It felt amazing! And then I was even more amazed to get an extra-special prize. Jody said, "We've decided to give a special award to someone who has shown the most improvement this week. So much, in fact, that she moved up a group. Sophie!"

Everyone clapped again, and when I looked over at Mum and Dad they were beaming the biggest smiles you could imagine.

When we came off the yard, I looked for

Beth and realized that while everyone was chatting to their families, she was leading Monsoon to the barn with Lydia. That's when I realized Jody was probably having a private word with her dad. I felt really sorry for Beth, but it was nice of Jody to wait till after the gymkhana, in case he was really angry.

I gave Shine a good brush down and took out her plaits, then got her some more fresh water even though she didn't really need any. I was just trying to delay saying goodbye for as long as possible! But in the end, I heard Mum calling me so I put my brushes away and flung my arms round Shine's neck. "Oh, Shine, thanks for being my wonderful pony for the week," I told her. "Even if I can't come back next year, and even if I'm ever lucky enough to get my own pony, I'll never forget you."

Shine whinnied and tossed her head, so I think that, somehow, she understood.

Just as I was bolting the stable door, Beth came over to me. "Dad wasn't furious after all," she said. "Just really worried about me."

I said, "That's good, but you will still tell him how you feel about things, won't you?"

Beth nodded, and we had a big goodbye hug. She's going to write to me and tell me what happens when they have the talk about his girlfriend moving in. Of course, nothing's ever perfect, but I think everything will work out okay for her.

I think things are going to work out okay for me too, actually. When we'd all said goodbye and I'd taken loads of pix and checked I'd got everything (and had a bit of a cry saying goodbye to Shine!) we finally got me and my stuff and Albie loaded into the car.

After we'd waved and waved to everyone and turned out into the road, Mum said, "I'm glad you had such a great time, but we really did miss you, Sophie. I don't know how I've coped without you this week. You're so helpful with the baby, I really do appreciate it. I'll take you riding more often from now on. We won't let all this improvement go to waste, I promise."

"Thanks, Mum," I said. "And I don't mind helping with Albie. He's okay, I suppose." I was amazed to hear myself say that, but I really meant it. It's taken a week away from my baby bro to make me realize I'm glad we've got him after all (even if he does cry a lot!). I don't feel like I want it to just be the three of us any more. "In fact, I think we should make our family even bigger," I said then.

"Oh, no way, I'm not having another one!" cried Mum.

"I wasn't talking about a baby," I giggled. "I'm thinking of a pony!"

Mum laughed then and Dad said, "We'll have

to see about that. Perhaps if you keep on improving as much as you have we could think about looking for a share. Maybe."

Wow! I couldn't believe he said they'd half-think about it – even for one second! I squealed so loudly it made Albie laugh. I know I'll have to prove I really deserve a pony, and show them how dedicated I am to my riding, but at least he didn't say absolutely no way!

I'm going to print out my pix now, well, after I've taken my dirty clothes downstairs and helped get Albie ready for bed. See, I've started being the perfect daughter already – that ought to help persuade them on the pony front! Tomorrow I'm planning to make a collage of my pictures from Sunnyside and put my rosettes on it too! And in the middle there'll be a big picture of me with Shine, my wonderful pony for the week!